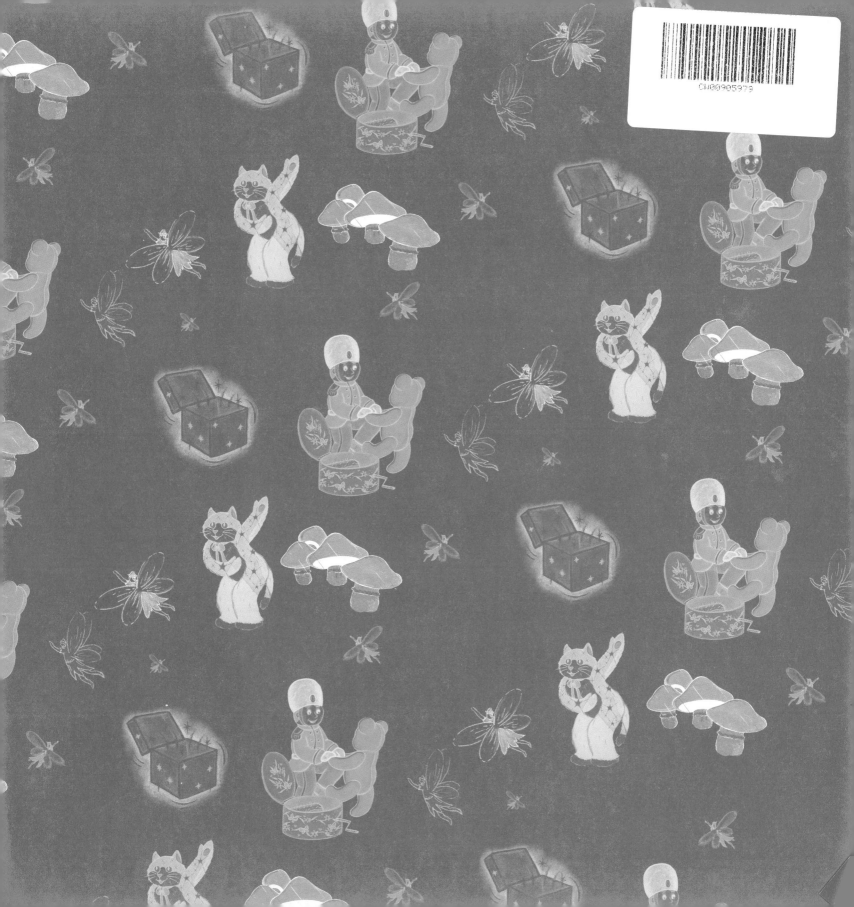

When Mrs Tumpy Lost Her Head

~ & ~

The Red-Spotted Handkerchief

Published in 2005 by Mercury Junior
20 Bloomsbury Street, London WC1B 3JH

© text copyright Enid Blyton Limited
© copyright original illustrations, Hodder and Stoughton Limited
© new illustrations 2005 Mercury Junior

Designed and produced for Mercury Junior
by Open Door Limited, Langham, Rutland

Title: When Mrs Tumpy Lost Her Head & The Red Spotted Handkerchief
ISBN: 1 904668 38 0

When Mrs Tumpy Lost Her Head

~ & ~

The Red-Spotted Handkerchief

Mercury
Junior

When Mrs Tumpy Lost Her Head

M rs Tumpy lived in Peppermint Village in a little cottage called Toffee Roofs. She was a fat, round goblin woman, and all the elves, pixies and goblins in the village used to laugh at her because she fussed so much.

If one of her hens got loose she would run for miles asking anyone if they had seen it – and maybe it was under her henhouse all the while!

If she cut her little finger she would cry and scream, and somebody else would have to bind it up for her because she was so upset.

And, dear me, one day when the wind caught her open umbrella and took her galloping down the village street, squealing for help, everyone thought she was being chased by robbers or something.

They came running out of their houses in fright. "Why, it's only that the wind has caught her open umbrella, like a ship's sail, and sent her scudding along," said Jinky, in disgust. "Hey, Mrs Tumpy – leave go the handle and you'll be all right."

But Mrs Tumpy was so scared that she quite lost her head. She wouldn't let go the umbrella handle, and the wind took her right to the duck-pond. She ran in at top speed and then sank. It took a long time to drag her out.

"Now, Mrs Tumpy," said Jinky, when she was drying in front of his fire. "Listen to me. You fuss too much. You lose your head at the smallest upset. You are always making people think that something dreadful is happening to you, and all the time it's only a spider that has come out of a corner and made you jump – or something like that."

"Don't talk to me like that," said Mrs Tumpy, crossly. "I won't have it."

"Well, you take my advice," said Jinky. "Don't lose your head too often – or one day it really will pop off and never come back!"

But Mrs Tumpy took no notice of his words at all, and she still went on squealing at nothing, making terrible fusses, and calling for help if she saw even an earwig.

So Jinky grinned a little grin to himself, and made up his mind to give Mrs Tumpy a shock. He went to his grandmother, Dame Know-a-Lot, and asked her for a disappearing spell. She gave him one in a box. It was blue powder.

"Whatever it's blown on will disappear," said Dame Know-a-Lot, It will still be there, of course, but no-one will see it. Take care how you use it, Jinky."

Now that afternoon Jinky walked quietly by Mrs Tumpy's garden. He peeped over the wall and saw what he had expected to see – Mrs Tumpy fast asleep in a deckchair.

Jinky smiled to himself. He jumped over the wall, and went on tiptoe to Mrs Tumpy. He took out his box of blue powder and blew it gently over her head. Then he went back over the wall.

14

He stood and watched. Mrs Tumpy's head gradually faded away and disappeared. How peculiar she looked! Jinky could still hear her snoring. He tiptoed away, smiling.

Mrs Tumpy soon woke up. She looked at her watch. Dear, dear, it was tea-time already.

And Dame Quickly was coming to tea!

Up she got and ran indoors. Soon she had
the kettle on and went to the
larder for the milk.

The cat had
been there
first. The
jug was
upset and the
milk was on the floor. Mrs Tumpy flew into a
rage, and began to fuss around angrily.

"Oh dear, dear, dear! Now what shall I do? No milk, and there's Dame Quickly coming to tea. No time to get any more. Oh, where's that cat! Tabby, Tabby, Tabby!"

The cat came, but she didn't hear it. She turned to go to the stove and fell over it. Crash! She knocked her best teapot off the table.

"Oh, my, look at that! Nothing but bad luck today. Now what am I to do? Oh, goodness knows how I shall ever get the tea ready at this rate."

There was a voice outside the front door and Mrs Tumpy heard the tap-tap-tap of Dame Quickly's stick as the old

lady walked into the hall. "Now, now, Mrs Tumpy, fussing again, and losing your head over something! Dear, dear."

Dame Quickly walked into the kitchen, and stopped in amazement, staring at Mrs Tumpy.

"What's the matter?" said Mrs Tumpy, crossly. "Haven't I done my hair?" She turned to look at herself in the big glass – and then she gave a scream of dismay.

"Where's my head? I've lost it! Oh, mercy me, what's happened to my head?"

"Oh, Mrs Tumpy, we always said you'd lose it if you went on like that," said Dame Quickly, "and now you have."

"Oh, oh – what shall I do? Where's my head gone?" wept Mrs Tumpy, and tears from where her head ought to be fell down the front of her dress. She looked all round the kitchen, but her head wasn't there. She even went and looked into the larder, but of course it was nowhere to be seen.

She ran out into the garden. "Has anyone seen my head?" she called to the astonished passers-by. "I've lost my head! Has anyone seen it?"

Now most people guessed at once that someone had put a spell on Mrs Tumpy to make her head invisible, and they laughed. But they weren't going to tell Mrs Tumpy why. Oh, dear me, no! Perhaps if she thought she really had lost her head, she wouldn't make such silly fusses as she did.

So everyone shook their heads, and said the same thing. "No, Mrs Tumpy – so sorry, but we haven't seen your head anywhere. Dear, dear, we always said you'd lose it if you went on kicking up such a fuss about everything."

Poor Mrs Tumpy couldn't eat any tea, or any supper either. She spent all the evening looking in the most unlikely places for her lost head. She even looked in the coal-scuttle and under the bed.

She went to bed very unhappy indeed. "I can't clean my teeth or brush my hair because my head has gone," she groaned. And then she was so tired out that she fell asleep.

In the night the spell wore off.

When she awoke and looked fearfully at
herself in the glass, how excited she was to
find that her head had come back again.
She smiled and nodded at it. "So you're back.
Welcome home to me! I am glad to see you.
And I do promise I'll never lose you again,
dear head, never, never, never!"

And she was very careful after that not to lose her head or fuss when anything went wrong. So Jinky's mischievous little spell did some good after all.

The Red-Spotted Handkerchief

Raggy the pixie had a red-spotted handkerchief that he was very proud of. It was a big one, with deep red spots all over it. Raggy always wore it in his front coat- pocket, where it stuck out a little so that everyone might see it.

Now one morning as Raggy was going along the road he wanted to sneeze. So he felt for his handkerchief to sneeze into – and it wasn't there!

Raggy was so surprised that he forgot to sneeze, which was a pity, for he really liked a good sneeze.

He stood there feeling anxiously in all his pockets, but it wasn't in any of them.

"Somebody must have taken it!" said Raggy. "Yes – somebody at the meeting I've just been to! Oh how naughty of them! I'll go straight back and see who's got it! They will still be there talking."

So back Raggy went and told everybody at the meeting that he had lost his red-spotted handkerchief.

"You lent it to Gobbo to wipe some spots off his coat," said Tag.

"But I gave it back!" said Gobbo at once.

"And you lent it to Hoppy to wave to his aunt when she passed by the window," said Tag.

"But I gave it back, I know I did!" said Hoppy.

He turned out his pockets, and certainly there was no handkerchief there.

"And I lent it to you, Tag, to polish your silver watch-chain this morning!" said Raggy. "You must have kept it."

"Indeed I didn't!" said Tag. "I put it back into your pocket myself. Did you lend it to anybody else?"

"Yes, Raggy lent it to me to pop over my head when I went out in the sun to look for Jiggy," said Chuffle. "I tied a knot in each corner – but I untied them when I came back, and gave the hanky back to Raggy. I know I did. It's no use looking at me like that, Raggy. I haven't got your handkerchief!"

"Well, it's a very funny thing," said Raggy, feeling angry. "I seem to have lent it to all of you this morning, and I haven't got it myself – so one of you must have kept it! It's very mean of you!"

"Very well, Raggy, we'll all turn out our pockets and show you that we haven't got it!" said Hoppy. And everyone turned out his pockets for Raggy to see. There were sweets and tops and string and money – but no red-spotted handkerchief.

"Now you turn out your pockets, Raggy!" said Hoppy. "We'll make quite sure you're not making all this fuss for nothing!"

So Raggy turned out his pockets, but there was no handkerchief there either.

"It's not a bit of use," said Raggy! "One of you has my beautiful handkerchief, and it's very wrong of you!"

"Now, Raggy, when you left the meeting, I know I saw your red handkerchief sticking out of your front coat-pocket," said Chuffle. "I just know I did. So if you took it away yourself, we couldn't have kept it! Did you

meet anyone
on your way
home?"
"No, nobody!"
said Raggy.

"Tell us exactly
what you did,"
said Hoppy.

"Well," said
Raggy, "I left the meeting, and walked up
the road. I met a dog with a black head,"

"Did you lend him your handkerchief?" asked Tag.

"No, of course not," said Raggy. "What would a dog want a handkerchief for? To wave to the engine-driver of the train, or something? Don't be silly."

"Well, go on," said Hoppy.

"And after a bit I saw a cow looking over a hedge," said Raggy.

40

"Did you lend her your handkerchief?" asked Chuffle.

"Really, Chuffle, do you suppose I go about lending cows my handkerchief?" said Raggy! "I suppose you think she wanted to polish her shoes with it? Well, she didn't!"

"Go on. What did you do next?" asked Hoppy.

"Well, let me see," said Raggy. "Oh, I know – a car came suddenly round the corner, and I had to jump quickly into the hedge – and I fell over and hurt my knee very badly."

"Did you really! Poor old Raggy," said Hoppy, for he knew how painful it was to fall down. "Did your knee bleed?"

"Oh, terribly!" said Raggy. "I had to bandage it..."

He suddenly stopped and went very red indeed. He didn't finish what he was going to say.

"Go on," said Tag. "Oh, that's all," said Raggy. "Well, I don't think I'll bother any more about my handkerchief. Good-bye, everyone."

"No, no, Raggy, don't go yet!" said Tag, and he held him by the arm. "Let's see your poor hurt knee!"

"Oh, it's quite all right now," said Raggy.

"It might not be," said Tag. "We'd better look and see if it wants bathing. Turn up your trouser leg, Raggy."

So Raggy had to, and his knee was neatly bound up with – what do you think? Yes – his red-spotted handkerchief!

"I don't wonder you feel ashamed of yourself," said Tag sternly. "Coming back here and making all that fuss, when if only you'd

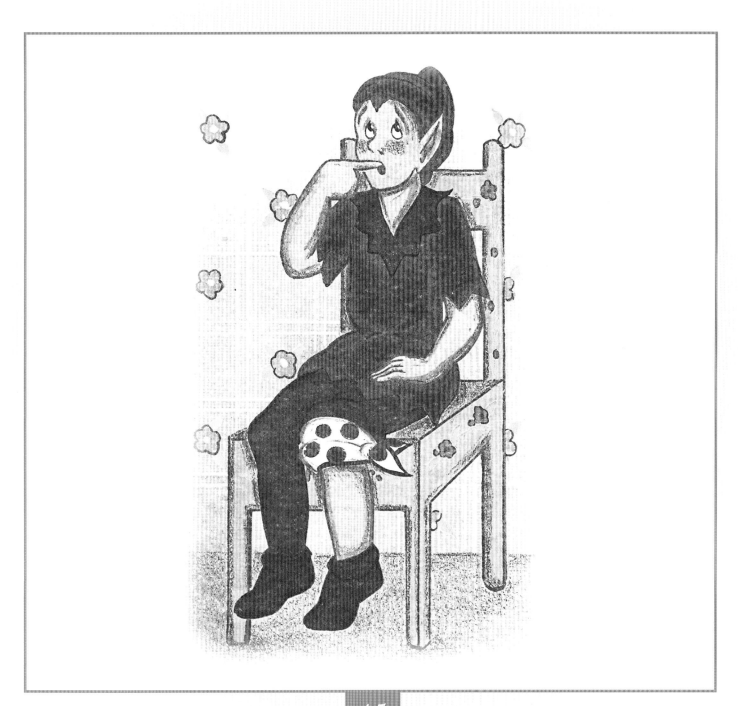

thought for a moment you'd have known quite well where your silly old handkerchief was all the time!"

"I'm sorry," said Raggy, and he went home feeling very much ashamed. He didn't like to wear his handkerchief any more, so now it is neatly folded in his drawer. Silly old Raggy – he did make a mistake, didn't he?

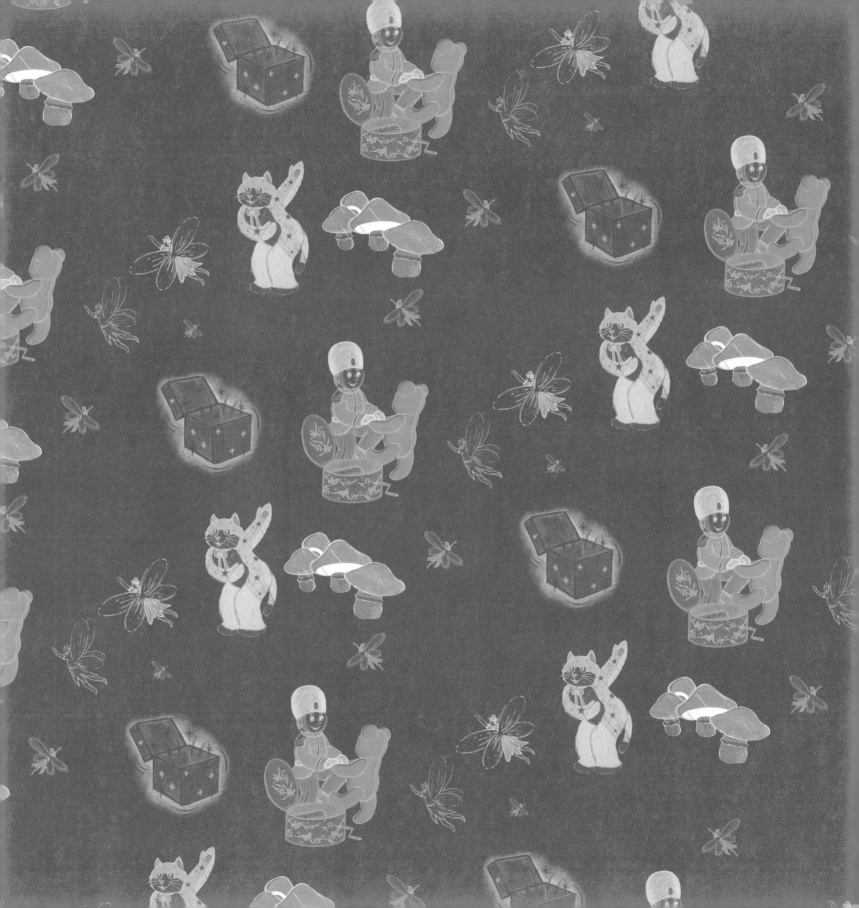